SCIENCE WITH
BATTERIES

Paul Shipton

Designed by Susie McCaffrey
Illustrated by Kate Davies
Series editor: Helen Edom
Consultant: Richard Hatton

Contents

Looking at batteries

Batteries make the electricity which works things like watches and toys. Look at the batteries in things around your house.

This radio uses four batteries.

Some watches need tiny batteries.

All batteries have a number with a V after it. The V stands for volts and the number is the battery's voltage. Batteries with a high voltage are stronger than batteries with a low voltage.

Which of your batteries has the highest voltage?

4·5V

1·5V

Light up

You need:
three 1·5 volt batteries,
2 pieces of plastic-covered wire *,
3·5 volt bulb in bulb holder *,
screwdriver,
scissors,
adhesive tape.

Ask an adult to strip about 2cm (1in) of plastic off each end of the wires.

The two metal ends of the battery are called terminals. One terminal is flat and one is button-shaped. Tape a wire to the flat terminal.

The metal wire must touch the flat terminal.

Screwdriver

Bulb

Hook the other end of the wire under a screw in the bulb holder. Screw it down with a screwdriver. Fasten the second wire under the other screw.

Bulb holder

Second wire

*You can buy these at an electrical shop or hardware store. Page 22 shows you which wires you can use.

Touch the free end of the second wire to the button terminal of the battery. The bulb lights because the battery pushes electricity through it.

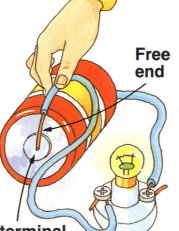

Free end

Button terminal

Tape the flat end of a second battery to the button end of the first battery. Touch the free wire to the button terminal of the second battery. What happens to the bulb?

Add a third battery and touch its button terminal with the free wire.

The bulb gets brighter and brighter because the batteries work together.

High voltage

Electricity from sockets in your house has a high voltage. It can be very dangerous. Only use batteries for your experiments.

Experiment batteries

For most experiments you can use three 1.5V batteries together, or one 4.5V battery. Here you can see some batteries with different terminals and how to join wires to them.

Wrap the wire ends around and tape them.

Hook wires around the terminals and screw the caps down.

4·5V

Tape wires to both ends.

3

Flowing around

Electricity only flows if it can get all the way around from one terminal of the battery to the other. The path it follows is called a circuit. When electricity flows in a circuit it is called current.

Flowing through

Electric current flows through some things but not others. To see what it can flow through, set up a battery, bulb and three wires like this.

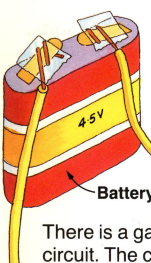

4·5 V

Battery

This wire joins the battery and bulb holder.

There is a gap in this circuit. The current cannot jump across the gap, so the bulb is not lit.

Gap   **Both of these wires are free at one end.**

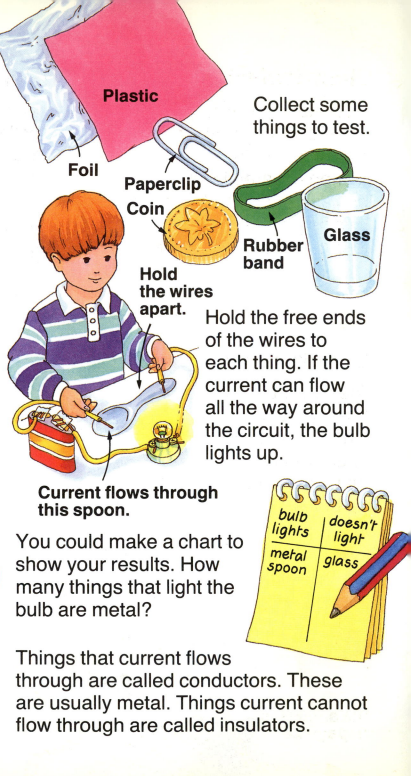

Plastic

Foil

Paperclip

Coin

Collect some things to test.

Rubber band

Glass

Hold the wires apart.

Hold the free ends of the wires to each thing. If the current can flow all the way around the circuit, the bulb lights up.

Current flows through this spoon.

You could make a chart to show your results. How many things that light the bulb are metal?

bulb lights | doesn't light
metal spoon | glass

Things that current flows through are called conductors. These are usually metal. Things current cannot flow through are called insulators.

Electrical wire

Most electrical wire is made of copper, which is a good conductor. It is often covered in an insulator such as plastic. This helps to make the electrical wire safe to use.

Pencil lead

There is a conductor called carbon in pencil lead. Some pencils have more carbon in them than others, so they are better conductors. See how bright the bulb is with different pencils.

Sharpen both ends.

Circuit maze

The current in this circuit flows through the foil. Which two corners would you touch with the wires to light the bulb?

You could make a circuit maze for your friends. Glue strips of foil onto cardboard. Make sure there is an unbroken path of foil between only two of the corners.

Foil

C

D

A

B

The answer is on page 24.

Inside a light bulb

Current can flow through a bulb because there are wires inside it. When it flows through a special coiled wire, the bulb lights.

Coiled wire

Wires

5

Turning on and off

You can make a switch for your circuits, to turn the lights on and off.

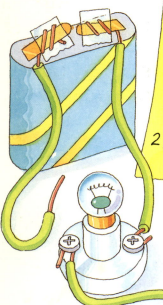

You need:
battery,
3 wires,
bulb in bulb holder,
small piece of cardboard,
paperclip,
2 paper fasteners,
adhesive tape.

Join a battery, bulb and three wires like this.*

Push a paper fastener through the cardboard. Hook the paperclip onto the second fastener and push this fastener through the cardboard.

Make sure the paperclip can touch the first fastener.

Turn the cardboard over. Wrap one wire around each paper fastener. Bend the legs of the fasteners back and tape them down.

The legs must not touch.

When the paperclip touches both fasteners, the circuit is complete. Electricity can flow through the clip and fasteners, so the bulb lights up.

The paperclip and fasteners are good conductors.

Move the paperclip off one fastener to switch off the bulb. The current cannot flow now because the circuit is broken.

Turn the light on and off with your switch.

*The same circuit is on page 4.

Scary face

Make a scary face to put over the bulb.

Turn a clear jar upside-down. Tape a see-through wrapper to one side.

Cut out a small face on a long piece of paper.

Tape the paper around the jar so the face is over the wrapper.

Cover the top with paper.

Fit the jar over the bulb. Turn the scary face light on and off with the switch.

Light hat

This light hat helps you to see in the dark.

Cut a cardboard strip long enough to go around your head so the ends overlap a little.

Set up a circuit with a switch on the cardboard like this. Tape everything down firmly.

You need: circuit with switch, plastic bottle (without cap), thin cardboard, foil, glue, adhesive tape.

Ask an adult to cut the top part off the bottle. Glue foil inside it. Tape the top over the bulb. Tape the ends of the cardboard together.

Bottle top

Foil

Tape

Switch

Battery

Bulb

Test your hat in the dark. Put it on your head and switch on the light.

7

Flashing light switch

There are lots of different kinds of switches. Here you can find out how to make a flashing light switch.

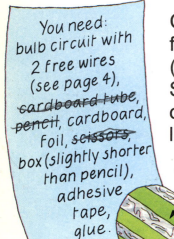

You need:
bulb circuit with
2 free wires
(see page 4),
~~cardboard tube,~~
~~pencil,~~ cardboard,
foil, ~~scissors,~~
box (slightly shorter
than pencil),
adhesive
tape,
glue.

Cut strips of foil about 2cm (1in) wide. Stick them onto the tube like this.

The tube must fit inside the box.

Leave spaces between the strips.

Cut cardboard circles to cover the ends. Make a hole in the middle of each circle. Tape them onto the ends of the tube. Push the pencil through the holes and tape it in place.

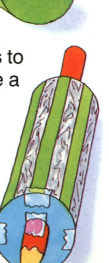

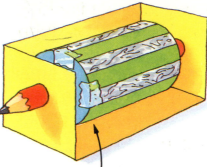

Make sure the tube doesn't touch the box.

Cut off part of the box so it looks like this. Make holes in the sides for the pencil to go through. Push the pencil through the holes.

Set up the bulb circuit as before. Ask an adult to strip 3cm (1½in) of plastic off the free ends of the wires.

Bare ends

Bend these free ends upward. Tape them to the box so the metal part touches the tube.

Turn this way.

Turn the pencil to make the light flash. When the wires touch the foil, the circuit is complete and the bulb lights. When the wires touch the cardboard, the current cannot flow.

Flashing lighthouse

Here is a way to use a flashing light switch. Make a large tube with thin cardboard and tape it to make the lighthouse tower.

You could paint the tube.

Make the switch as before. Tape a carboard circle to the top of the tube. Tape the bulb and holder to the top.

You need to use longer wires than usual.

Tape a clear jar over the bulb. Make the lighthouse flash with the switch.

You could make a paper roof.

Use blue paper for the sea.

Playdough rocks

Other switches

All switches work by completing and breaking circuits.

Some switches are hidden. When someone opens this refrigerator door, a switch completes the circuit, so the light comes on.

Each key on a computer keyboard is a simple switch that controls a complicated circuit.

Pressing a key completes a circuit.

Other circuits

In these circuits the battery lights two bulbs at once.

Bulbs in a row

Join a wire to each battery terminal. Fasten a bulb and holder to each wire.

Join the bulb holders with a third wire so the bulbs light.

Are the lights as bright as usual?

The bulbs are dim because the current goes through one bulb and then the other. The battery has to work hard to light them both.

Take one bulb out of its holder.* You have broken the circuit, so the other bulb goes out.

This is called a series circuit.

*Never touch household bulbs when they are lit.

Brighter bulbs

Start by joining a wire to each terminal. Then twist two short wires onto the free end of each wire.

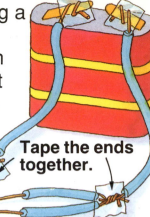

Tape the ends together.

Join a bulb and holder to each short wire on one side.

Christmas lights

Christmas tree lights are often in a series circuit. One broken bulb can stop the others from lighting.

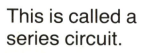

Fasten the short wires on the other side to the bulb holders. How bright are the bulbs now?

The bulbs are bright because they are on different paths. The current only has to flow through one bulb on each path to get around the circuit.

Take one bulb out of its holder. What happens to the other bulb?

When you take out one bulb, the other stays lit. The current has another path to flow around the circuit.

This is a parallel circuit.*

*To stop your battery from running down, take the bulbs out.

Owl light

Draw an owl on cardboard and cut it out. Stick down circles of foil for the eyes. Push a pencil through them to make a hole in each eye.

You need: your parallel circuit, cardboard, foil, scissors, pencil, glue, adhesive tape.

The owl should be much larger than your battery.

Back of bulb holders

Tape

Take the bulbs out of the holders. Tape the circuit to the back of the owl so the holders poke through the eyeholes.

Screw the bulbs into the holders to turn on the light.

11

Making sound

Electricity does not just make light. It can make sound as well. Light and sound are both different kinds of energy.

Buzzer circuit

You can make sound with this circuit. You need a 6V buzzer, which you can buy at an electrical store.

Join a wire between one battery terminal and one of the buzzer wires. Join a second wire to the other side of the buzzer.

Free wire

Twist the wires together and tape them.

Other energy

Heat and movement are other kinds of energy that electricity can produce.

An electric motor makes this toy move.

Electricity makes heat in an electric iron.

Touch the free wire to the second terminal to set the buzzer off.

If your buzzer does not work, untwist the wires, turn the buzzer around and join it up again.

Buzzers make sound by making a thin metal strip shake very quickly. This movement is called vibration. You can feel it if you touch the buzzer.

Make a buzzer game

Set up a buzzer circuit. Then join a third wire to the battery, so there are two free ends in the circuit.

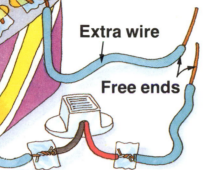

Extra wire

Free ends

Cover the bottom of the matchbox tray with foil and tape the free end of one wire to it. Tape the other wire to a piece of foil. Lay the foil over the matchbox.

Cut a slot in one end of the shoebox lid. Fit the tube into it.

Shoebox lid

Cut off the other end of the lid. Stick cotton reels* to the lid as obstacles.

Put two reels here.

Put books under both ends of the lid. The end with the tube should be higher.

This end is cut off.

Put the matchbox and circuit in front of the lower end of the lid.

Roll a marble through the tube, aiming it down the lid. If it lands in the matchbox, it knocks the pieces of foil together and completes the circuit. Can you set off the buzzer?

*Spools of thread (US)

13

Electricity and water

Electricity can flow through water. You can set up a circuit with water like this.

You need:
bulb circuit with 2 free wires (see page 4), bowl of water, foil, salt.

Cut two large squares of foil. Hook each free wire in the circuit onto a square.

Put the foil squares into the water. Does the bulb light?

Don't let the squares touch.

A little current flows through the water, but not enough to light the bulb.

Socket electricity

Electricity from sockets has such a high voltage that it can flow through tap water easily. Never touch plugs or sockets with wet hands.

Stir in four big spoonfuls of salt. What happens?

Mixing salt and water makes a good conductor. Enough current flows through it to light the bulb.

Now use your circuit to see if electricity flows through dry salt. Does the bulb light?

Current flows through salty water, but dry salt is not a conductor.

Electrical timer

Try making an electrical timer, using salty water as a conductor.

You need:
wire, tall jar, salty water,
buzzer circuit (see page 12),
2 foil squares, adhesive tape,
empty dishwashing
liquid bottle.

Set up the buzzer circuit. Join an extra wire to the battery so there are two free wires. Hook each free end onto a foil square and hang them in the jar.

Tape

Extra wire

Leave about 7cm (3in) at the bottom.

Ask an adult to cut the bottle in half. Fill the top half with salty water.

Keep the cap on.

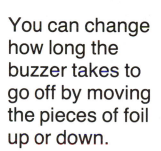

Open the cap and place the bottle over the jar. The salty water runs into the jar. When it reaches the foil, it completes the circuit and the buzzer goes off.

You can change how long the buzzer takes to go off by moving the pieces of foil up or down.

When the foil is higher, the timer takes longer.

You can use your timer for a game. Hide something. Can your friends find it before the buzzer goes off?

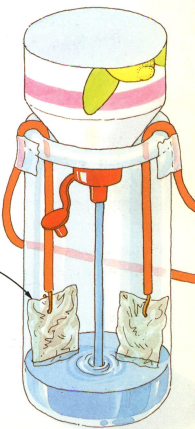

15

Making magnets

Electricity can turn iron or steel into magnets. You can use your battery to make a magnet like this.

You need:
battery and 2 wires, 2m (6½ft) of thin wire (see page 23), bulb and holder, switch (see page 6), iron nail, adhesive tape, paperclip.

Wrap the thin wire tightly around the nail as many times as you can.

Tape the wire in place.

Hold the nail near a paperclip and turn on the switch. What happens?

The current makes the coil of wire magnetic. This turns the nail into a magnet, so it picks up the clip.

The bulb shows when the nail magnet is working.

Join the other wires to the battery terminals. Fasten one to the bulb holder and one to the switch.

Join one end of the wire around the nail to the switch, and the other to the bulb holder.

Turn off the switch. The clip falls off because the coil is only magnetic when current is flowing through it.*

Magnets made by electricity are called electromagnets. They are very useful because you can turn them on and off.

*The nail may still be a little magnetic. You can find out why on page 23.

16

Target game

You can make this target game with your electromagnet.

You also need: playdough, paperclips, box, paper, crayons.

Make four small balls of playdough. Stick a paperclip into each one.

Draw a target. Number the rings like this.

Turn the box upside-down and put your circuit on it. Pick up each ball with the electromagnet. Hold it over the target and turn the switch off, so the ball falls onto the target.

If the ball does not fall at once, shake the nail.

The number in the ring where each ball lands gives your score.

Making electricity

Magnets are used to make electricity. When a magnet moves near a coil of wire, it makes electric current flow in the wire.

Bike lights

In a bicycle dynamo, the wheel turns a magnet near a coil. This makes current to light the lamp.

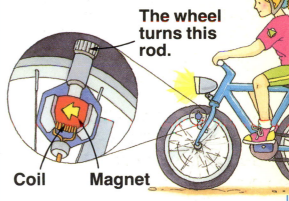

The wheel turns this rod.

Coil   **Magnet**

Generators

Electricity for houses is made in power stations by giant dynamos. They are called electric generators.

Power station

Batteries and meters

You can make a current meter using a compass. It shows when even a little electricity is flowing.

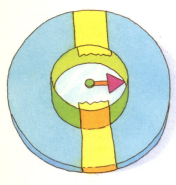

Cut two slots in the cardboard. Wind the wire tightly around the compass at least 50 times.

Tape the compass to a cardboard circle.

You need: small compass, 2m (6 ½ ft) of thin wire (see page 23), cardboard, battery, scissors, adhesive tape.

Wind the wire inside the slots.

Join the wire ends to a battery. The current flows through the wire and makes it magnetic. This makes the compass needle move.

*You can get a washer from a hardware store.

Make a battery

You can make a battery of your own. It is not strong enough to light a bulb, but you can test it with the current meter you have made.

You need: steel washer*, vinegar, coffee filter paper, shiny bronze coin, scissors, saucer.

Cut a circle of filter paper as big as the washer. Soak it in vinegar.

Filter paper

Press the steel washer, paper, and bronze coin together.

Touch one wire from your meter to the washer and the other to the coin. The compass needle moves. This shows that the battery is making current.

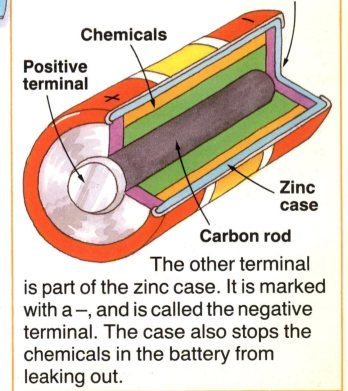

Inside batteries

All batteries work like your home-made battery. Chemicals and two different conductors work together to make electricity.*

In this battery the two conductors are carbon and zinc. The carbon rod is joined to the terminal with + on it. This is called the positive terminal.

Negative terminal

Chemicals

Positive terminal

Zinc case

Carbon rod

The steel and bronze are both conductors. The chemicals in the vinegar work together with them to make electric current. This only happens when the battery is in a circuit.

You can make the battery stronger by adding extra washers, paper and coins.

Put the layers in the same order.

The other terminal is part of the zinc case. It is marked with a −, and is called the negative terminal. The case also stops the chemicals in the battery from leaking out.

Never try to look inside a battery. The chemicals are dangerous.

Bright ideas

You can make lots of things using what you have learned about electricity.

Frog game

This game uses the idea that current only flows around a complete circuit (see page 4).

You need:
battery, wires,
6V buzzer (see page 12),
paper fasteners, thin cardboard,
crayons, scissors, adhesive tape.

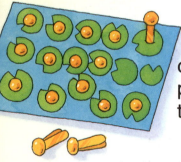

Draw lots of lily pads on the cardboard. Push paper fasteners through them.

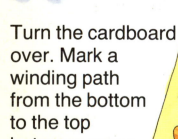

Turn the cardboard over. Mark a winding path from the bottom to the top between some fasteners.

Join short wires between the other fasteners. Fasten the last wire to a battery terminal. Join the other terminal and the buzzer with a wire.

Join a long wire to the buzzer. Tape a paper frog shape to the free end.

The wire should stick out.

Turn the cardboard over. Try to get from the bottom to the top by moving the frog wire from one fastener to the next. The buzzer goes off if you land on a pad outside the path. When this happens, go back to the bottom and start again.

The wire must touch the fasteners.

Moon buggy

You can use the flashing light switch (page 8) in this buggy. Make the tube for the switch as before, but do not tape the pencil to the cardboard. This picture shows you how to make the buggy.

The light flashes when you push the buggy along.

Let the nails hang down onto the front roller.

Flag

Tape cardboard together to make the sides and top.

The back roller is a switch tube without foil strips.

Push the pencils through the sides. Stop them from turning with playdough.

Tape down the bulb circuit.

Wind each bare end around a nail*.

Foil strips on switch.

You could put a painted cardboard box over the buggy to turn it into a toy fire engine.

Hole for bulb

Cardboard box

Be an inventor
Can you think of other ways to change or improve the things you have made?

A switch here makes the owl on page 11 wink.

*Copper nails work best.

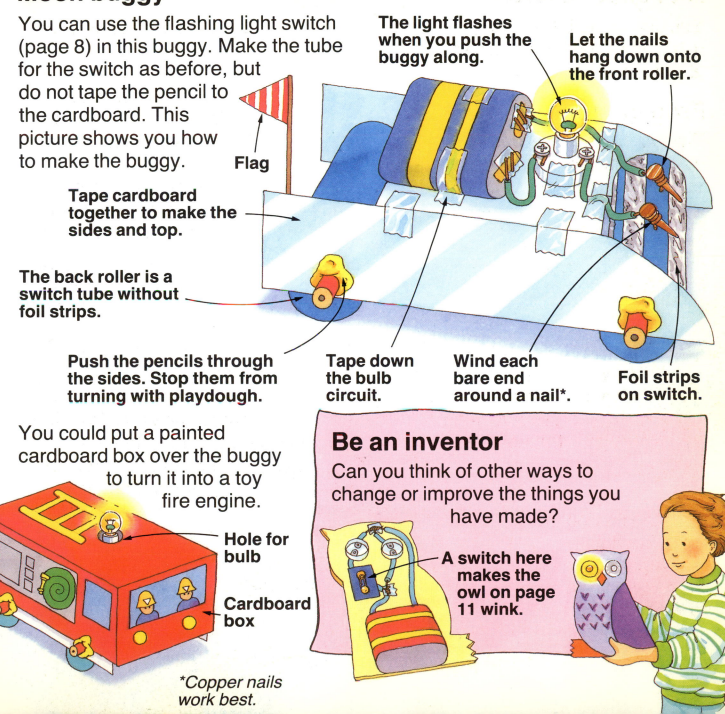

Notes for parents and teachers

These notes will help to answer questions that arise from the activities on earlier pages.

Equipment

A battery that is too strong can burn out a bulb. This chart shows the right bulbs to use with different batteries.

Battery	Bulb
1·5 V	1·1 – 1·5 V
4·5 V (or three 1·5 V batteries together)	3 – 4·5 V
6 V	5 – 6·5 V

Use low voltage wire (not wire for household electricity). Here are some kinds of wire you can use.

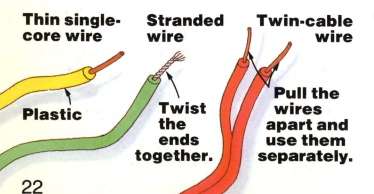

Thin single-core wire

Plastic

Stranded wire

Twist the ends together.

Twin-cable wire

Pull the wires apart and use them separately.

Looking at batteries (pages 2-3)

Electricity flowing through a wire is a stream of tiny invisible particles called electrons. A battery's voltage is a measure of how hard it pushes the electrons around a circuit.

Flowing around (pages 4-5)

Carbon is a conductor, although it is not a metal. Soft pencils – ones that produce darker lines – contain more carbon, so they are better conductors than hard pencils.

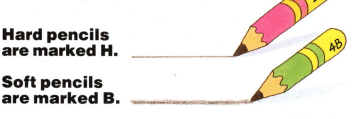

Hard pencils are marked H.

Soft pencils are marked B.

Bulbs

All conductors oppose, or resist, current to some extent. Thin wire resists current more than thick wire. The coiled wire inside bulbs, called the filament, is very thin, so it is difficult for current to flow through it. This makes the filament heat up and glow.

The filament glows white when it is hot.

Making sound (pages 12-13)

Sound, light, heat, movement and electricity are all forms of energy. Energy cannot be created or destroyed; it can only be turned into other forms of energy. Electricity is easy to turn into other kinds of energy.

Electricity and water (pages 14-15)

When things dissolve in water they split into tiny particles called ions. Ions can carry electrons through the water and complete a circuit. Tap water has small amounts of chemicals in it, so it contains ions. This means it can conduct electricity, but not as well as salty water.

Making magnets (pages 16-17)

You must use a bulb to make the electromagnet circuit safe. It stops the wires from getting too hot.

To make an electromagnet (and the current meter on page 18) use very thin covered wire. Thin plastic-covered wire called hook-up wire works well. Glazed copper wire, or magnet wire, is particularly good.

Glazed copper wire

Rub the ends with sandpaper until they are shiny.

Wires generate a magnetic field when current flows through them. Making the wire into a coil, or solenoid, strengthens the magnetic field. An iron or steel core, such as a nail, makes the field even stronger. The field turns the core into a magnet. Steel and some kinds of iron can stay magnetic even when the current is turned off.

Batteries and meters (pages 18-19)

Compass needles are magnets that normally point north/south. When one is near a solenoid, the needle reacts to its magnetic field.

Inside batteries

When the battery is in a circuit, a chemical reaction starts between the chemicals and the two conductors inside the battery. This produces ions which carry electrons to the negative terminal. The electrons travel around the circuit to the positive terminal.

The electrons move along the wire.

Index

Answer to puzzle on page 5

Touch the wires to corners C and D to complete the circuit and light the bulb.

First published in 1992 by Usborne Publishing Ltd, Usborne House, 83-85 Saffron Hill, London, EC1N 8RT, England. Copyright © 1992 Usborne Publishing Ltd.

First published in America March 1993